THE
GREAT TEAM
OMNIBUS

Four Books

Rob Childs

Illustrated by Michael Reid

www.kidsatrandomhouse.co.uk

FOR MY GREAT MUM!

THE GREAT TEAM OMNIBUS
A CORGI PUPS BOOK 0 552 55225 9

First published as separate editions in Great Britain
in 1998, 1999, 2000 and 2001 by Corgi Pups,
an imprint of Random House Children's Books

This 4-in-1 edition published 2005

3 5 7 9 10 8 6 4

Set in 18/25 pt Bembo Schoolbook

Corgi Pups are published by Random House Children's Books,
61–63 Uxbridge Road, London W5 5SA,
a division of The Random House Group Ltd,
in Australia by Random House Australia (Pty) Ltd,
20 Alfred Street, Milsons Point, Sydney, NSW 2061, Australia,
in New Zealand by Random House New Zealand Ltd,
18 Poland Road, Glenfield, Auckland 10, New Zealand,
and in South Africa by Random House (Pty) Ltd,
Isle of Houghton, Corner of Boundary Road & Carse O'Gowrie,
Houghton 2198, South Africa

THE RANDOM HOUSE GROUP Limited Reg. No. 954009
www.kidsatrandomhouse.co.uk

A CIP catalogue record for this book is available from the British Library.

Printed and bound in Great Britain by
Cox & Wyman Ltd, Reading, Berkshire

CONTENTS

Series Reading Consultant: Prue Goodwin,
Lecturer in literacy and children's books,
University of Reading

GREAT
SAVE!

Chapter One

As the children arrived at the village school, they gazed proudly at the long, colourful banner hanging above the main door.

"It looks brilliant!" cried Hannah.

"It should do," said Tom. "We spent ages painting it."

Rebecca sighed. "I'll be very sad if our little school really has to close."

"No more school . . ." Tom said dreamily. "I could stay in bed all day!"

"They won't let you do that," Rebecca said, pulling a face. "We'd have to go to that big horrible school in town instead."

"By bus!" Hannah said in disgust. "Yuk!"

Michael came into the
playground to ring the bell.
CLANG! CLANG! DING!
DONG!

"OK, OK, Michael, we've heard it," Tom grinned. "I reckon you've woken up the whole of Great Catesby by now."

The small group of seven- and eight-year-olds sat on the carpet around their teacher.

"We're going to have a new boy in our class today," Mrs Roberts told them. "He wasn't very happy at his old school, so let's make sure that he will like it here with us."

Michael put his hand up. "He won't be here for long if the place is gonna close soon!" he said cheekily.

The teacher frowned at him. "We'll all be doing our best to stop that from happening."

"But how can we stop it?" Hannah blurted out.

"It won't be easy," Mrs Roberts admitted. "But we mustn't give up hope of finding a way to save our lovely school."

Rebecca couldn't help bursting into song. It was the latest hit single by her favourite pop star, the Red Fox.

"Never give up, never give up,
   Stop your crying, you gotta keep
on trying,
   Something will turn up — will
always turn up . . ."

The others joined in the chorus.
   "Something will turn up — will
always turn up . . ."

Something did at that very moment. With the children in full voice, the classroom door was pushed open and Miss Jackson, the headteacher, walked in.

The song faded away as, one by one, they stared at the little boy with ginger hair standing next to her. He had a football tucked under his arm.

"I wish you would all sing as well as that in assembly," Miss Jackson said with  a smile and then introduced their new classmate. "This is Jonty. Say hello, everyone."

The boy gave them a wide, toothy grin and the ice was broken.

"Hello, Jonty!" they chorused.

"Hi!" he beamed, and suddenly bounced the ball on the floor. "Anybody here like to play football?"

They all laughed. "Welcome, Jonty," Mrs Roberts greeted him warmly. "It seems like you've come to the right place. This lot of mine are totally soccer-mad."

Chapter Two

Jonty's arrival at Great Catesby was well timed. Mrs Roberts was planning to enter a class team in a five-a-side football tournament especially for their age-group.

"You live in that big house outside the village, don't you?" Michael said to him one day. "Are your parents rich?"

Jonty gave a shrug. "Haven't got a mum. And Dad's away a lot. I don't see much of him."

"Who looks after you then?"
asked Rebecca, trying to work
out what it was about Jonty
that seemed so familiar to her.

"Gran does," he said. "And
we've got a housekeeper too."

"I'd rather be a goalkeeper!"
grinned Hannah.

★

The first practice for the Fives
was held later that week
Most of the class took part,
hoping to be picked for the
team.

"It will be mixed, won't it?"
asked Hannah. "Girls too."

"Of course," said Mrs Roberts.
"You're our best goalie."

"Out of all the girls, maybe,"
Imran whispered to Tom. "But
not the best in the whole class.
That's me."

"You'll have to prove it,
Imran," Tom smirked. "She's
good."

Jonty took his own leather
ball to the practice and he was
the first one to score with it as
well. His shot was low and hard
and the ball fizzed just out of
reach of Hannah's dive.

Hannah was more upset by Imran's laughter at the other end than she was at letting the goal in. And she soon made up for it. She saved another effort from Jonty and then stopped a close-range header from Tom on the line.

Hannah threw the ball out to
Rebecca on the wing to start
their own team's next attack.

Rebecca had won the sprint
race on Sports Day and was too
quick for anyone to catch her,
even running with the ball at
her feet.

She curled the ball over into the goalmouth, but it floated right into Imran's arms. Or at least it should have done. Imran took his eye off the ball at the last moment and let it slip between his legs into the goal. He was so embarrassed, he held his head in his hands.

"Careful, Imran!" yelled Tom. "You might drop that too!"

Imran decided he didn't want to play in goal after all. He was better out on the pitch as a defender.

When the practice finished,
Rebecca had a sudden
brainwave. "Why don't we ask
people to sponsor us in the
Fives?" she suggested. "We
could raise a lot of money for
the school."

"Great idea!" said Tom. "But what about kit? We can't all wear different colours."

"That is a problem," agreed Mrs Roberts. "I'm afraid the school can't afford to buy a team strip."

"I'll see if my dad might be able to help," Jonty piped up, making himself even more popular. "He's a big football fan."

Rebecca nodded. "I bet that's not all he is either," she said under her breath.

A wild rumour had begun to snake around the village that a famous pop star had recently moved into the area. Nobody thought that it could possibly be true — apart from Rebecca . . .

Chapter Three

The children could not believe their eyes. A man with bright red hair had just walked into their classroom.

But it wasn't his hair colour that gave them such a shock. It was because they recognized him. He was the Red Fox!

Only Mrs Roberts and Jonty were expecting his visit.

The Red Fox was holding a large cardboard box. "Got some stuff here for all you star footballers," he said with a grin.

The pop star tipped the box upside down and lots of soccer kit tumbled out on to the floor.

He grabbed one of the red shirts
and held it up for everyone to
see.

It had a big white capital G
on the front and the name
GREATS printed across the
back above the number.

"G is for Great — and that's what you'll be in the Fives!" he cried before breaking into a chant. *"C'mon, you Greats! C'mon, you Greats!"*

The children were still too stunned to know what to do until Rebecca joined in and then the rest followed. Their loud chanting echoed around the school – and probably halfway around Great Catesby as well.

"C'mon, you Greats! C'mon, you Greats!"

When the Red Fox had gone, Jonty was surrounded.

"Is he really your dad?" Tom demanded. "You could have told us!"

Jonty smiled shyly. "I wanted

to keep it a secret for a while. I
hoped you wouldn't all be
friends with me just because of
who my dad is."

"With your name being Fox
and your ginger hair, we should
have guessed," said Hannah.

"I already did," Rebecca claimed. "And last night I found I've even got a picture of Jonty in my Red Fox scrapbook. I knew I'd seen him somewhere before."

"Becky's fallen in love with Jonty!" Imran teased her. Rebecca ignored him.

"Incredible!" she sighed. "I've just been singing along with the Red Fox!"

"He's only Jonty's dad," Imran sneered.

"*Only!*" she sneered back. "He's the best pop singer in the world."

"Well, my dad sings pretty well too – in the bath."

"Yeah, but I don't have a poster of your dad on my bedroom wall," she laughed. "Especially not one of him in the bath!"

★

After another soccer practice, Mrs Roberts chose a squad of six players for the tournament so that they had a substitute for each game. She wrote the names on the entry form.

FIVE-A-SIDE COMPETITION
- Entry Form -
Tom (captain) Hannah Rebecca
Jonty Michael Imran

The whole school had a special reason for hoping that the team did well. The Red Fox was so pleased by how quickly Jonty had settled in that he was sponsoring the Greats too.

Not just for a few pence per goal. Not even for a pound a goal like some generous people in the village. But for as much as a thousand pounds for every goal that they scored!

Jonty's only disappointment
was that his dad wouldn't be
able to watch them play in the
Fives. He was setting off on a
concert tour with his band.

"I'll be thinking of you, Jonty-boy," his dad promised before he left. "Show 'em who's the soccer star of the Fox family."

Jonty managed a weak smile.

"I really like it at this school, Dad. If it's closed, I might have to go back to that horrible boarding school where I was bullied."

"There'll be no going back there, don't worry. I'll see to that, OK?"

"C'mon, you Greats!" they sang happily together.

Chapter Four

"Fantastic! We're in the quarter-finals now," cried Tom.

The captain's second goal
had just clinched his team's 2–0
victory, their third win in a row.

The Greats were enjoying themselves so much, they'd almost forgotten about all the money they were earning for the school.

"Wish my dad could have been here to see us," said Jonty.

There was a sudden stir of excitement in the crowd as a helicopter began to circle overhead. It looked as if it was going to land on the playing fields.

It did. Everyone felt the gusts
of wind from the whirling
blades, and then a red-haired
figure in a white suit stepped
down from the helicopter and
ran towards them.

The Red Fox was soon surrounded by autograph-hunters.

"Hope I'm not too late," he called out to the Greats.

Inspired by his flying visit, they hit top form and the red shirts swarmed all over their opponents in the next match.

Goals from Rebecca, Michael
and Jonty swept them easily into
the semi-finals.

"*C'mon, you
Greats!*" cheered
their fans, led
by the Red
Fox himself. He
jumped nearly as high as his
helicopter when Jonty scored the
third goal!

 "You're costing me a fortune," he laughed, clearly not minding one little bit.

The semi-final game was much tougher. The score was locked at 0–0 until the last minute, and that's when Hannah pulled off a magnificent save to rescue her team.

A goal looked certain. A shot was deflected off Imran's knee, but Hannah twisted round and hurled herself through the air to fingertip the ball over the crossbar.

"What a save!" cried Imran. "Thanks, Hannah. I take back all I've said. You're magic in goal!"

Tom headed the corner out of danger towards Rebecca and the Greats launched a swift breakaway raid. As Rebecca raced up the pitch, Jonty matched her for pace and he burst past his marker to reach her pass first. He smacked the ball from just outside the keeper's area and it screamed into the goal.

Jonty disappeared under a pile of teammates as they mobbed him. Only Hannah stayed out of the crush of bodies.

"We're in the Final!" she yelled. "We've made it!"

There wasn't much time for the players to rest before the Final, but they were too excited to feel tired yet. They were up against the tournament favourites, the Fab Five, a strong team from the biggest school in the county.

The Greats didn't care who they were playing. They rocked the Fab Five straight from the kick-off when Imran's long-range shot whistled only a fraction wide of the target. And

with a little luck, they might
have been leading by more than
1–0 at half-time. Rebecca
scored their goal, sliding home
the rebound after Tom's volley
had struck a post.

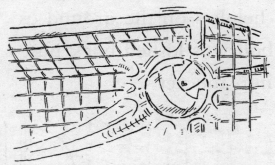

The second half, sadly, told a
different story. Once the Fab
Five had equalized, the Greats
struggled to survive a storm of
fierce attacks. Just when it

looked like they might hang on
for a draw, their defence was
finally cracked.

Not even Hannah could keep
out the winning goal. She'd
already blocked one shot and
was helpless on the ground as
the ball was lashed back past
her into the net.

"Never mind," said Mrs Roberts after the squad received their silver medals as runners-up. "You all played your best and nobody can ask for more than that."

"But we didn't win," sighed Rebecca, almost in tears, despite the fact that they'd scored a total of ten goals.

"Cheer up!" said the Red Fox.
"There's always another day."

"Not for our school, there
won't be," grunted Tom.

The pop star began to sing.

"Never give up, never give up,
Something will turn up, will
always turn up . . ."

"I know what can turn up, Dad," cried Jonty. "A song! Why don't you make a record with all the kids at Great Catesby? That could raise loads more money to help save the school."

Everyone thought that was a wonderful idea — including the Red Fox. He ruffled his son's ginger hair.

"Right, let's do it, Jonty-boy," he grinned. "If it did the trick, it'd be an even greater save than Hannah's!"

Jonty started up their chant again and the footballers really had something to sing about now. Mrs Roberts laughed in delight. "It sounds like we've got the title for our song already!"

"*C'mon, you Greats! C'mon, you Greats!*"

THE END

GREAT
SHOT!

Chapter One

"Have a go! Shoot!"

Tom shot – low and hard. The ball zipped over the grass but scraped the wrong side of the goalpost and went out of play.

Mrs Roberts called out again. "Good try, Tom. Better luck next time."

The teacher glanced at her watch and saw that it was nearly the end of the game.

"Looks like we're going to lose," she sighed. "Pity! All six have played so well as a team."

Hannah had pulled off a
number of fine saves in goal . . .

Imran and Michael had made
some good tackles in defence . . .

Jonty and Rebecca had fired
lots of shots in attack . . .

And captain Tom's passing
had been excellent in
midfield . . .

But nobody had yet been able
to put the ball in the back of the
net.

Their friends on the touchline refused to give up hope. "*C'mon, you Greats!*" they chanted. "*C'mon, you Greats!*"

Two of them waved a painted banner in the air. Its bright red letters displayed the same message for everyone to see.

It was also the title of a new song written by the pupils of Great Catesby Primary School.

A famous pop star, the Red Fox, was going to sing along with them to help raise enough money to save their small village school from being closed.

The Red Fox's son was on the ball now. Jonty dribbled past two defenders before passing to Rebecca who was unmarked just outside the goal area.

The Greats' leading scorer controlled the ball, took steady aim and calmly stroked it home. Then Rebecca totally lost her cool.

"GOOAALL!!" she screamed at the top of her voice.

Rebecca danced away in delight until she was caught and mobbed by her teammates. Even Hannah ran up to join in the celebrations.

"At last!" Jonty yelled. "Great goal, Becky!"

"C'mon, we've still got time to grab the equalizer," Tom urged.

Sadly, it wasn't to be their day. They only had one more chance to score, but Tom miskicked and scooped the ball over the crossbar.

"Three cheers for Great
Catesby!" cried the winning
captain at the final whistle. "Hip,
hip – hooray!"

A disappointed Tom led his
team's response, but his heart
wasn't really in it. He blamed
himself for their 2–1 defeat.

"I should have had a hat-trick today," he moaned.

"I think we all need some extra shooting practice," said Jonty. "We must start getting more of our shots on target."

Chapter Two

The following Saturday
morning, as arranged, Tom
arrived at Great Catesby
Manor. The old house, standing
in its own private grounds just
outside the village, was the new
home of the Red Fox.

"Cool!" he exclaimed as Jonty met him on the front lawn. "You're dead lucky, having all this space to play in."

Jonty gazed around the large gardens, as if seeing them for the first time himself. "Yeah, guess so," he said, nodding. "I just wish Dad wasn't away on tour so much with his band."

"Well, anyway, now I'm here,
let's get our shooting boots on,"
said Tom, eager for action.

"Shooting boots?"

"That's what my dad always
calls them. 'Don't forget your
shooting boots,' he says, every
match day."

"You must have left them at home last time," said Jonty cheekily.

The boys chalked a small goal on the wall of one of the garages and divided it up into eight large squares for target practice.

"Glad to see you can count up to eight!" Jonty joked as Tom finished drawing a number in each of the boxes.

"Huh! Very funny," snorted the captain. "Bet I can hit all eight as well before you do. And we have to hit them in the right order, OK?"

"OK, so long as I can start. It's my ball."

Jonty took five attempts to get off the mark. But even that was better than Tom who needed nine goes before he belted the ball into box 1.

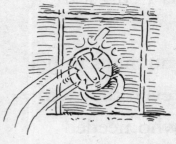

Their aim gradually improved with practice. Tom struck the last three boxes in a row to snatch victory 8–6, but Jonty easily

won the second game. His final shot was superb, curling and dipping into the bottom corner of the goal.

Jonty celebrated with a chorus
of the school's special song.

"*C'mon, you Greats!*

C'mon, you Greats!

Come and watch us win

our games,

Come and shout out all our

names.

C'mon, you Greats!

C'mon, you Greats!"

"You sing better than the Red
Fox," laughed Tom. "Has he
heard it yet?"

"Yeah, I sang it to him on the phone last week. He thinks it's *great*!" Jonty giggled. "He wants us to record it as soon as he comes home."

The deciding contest had to wait. The ball had gone flat after its constant pounding against the brickwork.

"Must be all my cannonball shooting!" boasted Tom.

"No problem," said Jonty. He nipped into the house and soon came back out with another ball.

"How many have you got?" asked Tom, trying not to sound envious.

Jonty shrugged. "Oh, a few. C'mon, let's kick off again."

Tom went into an early 2–0 lead, but Jonty managed to catch up and level the scores at seven each. It could not have been closer.

At that moment, a police car
turned through the manor's iron
gates and scrunched to a halt in
the gravel. A sergeant climbed
out and walked towards the
footballers.

Jonty looked worried, fearing something bad might have happened, but Tom took the chance to show off. He crashed the ball straight into box 8 and grinned at the policeman.

"Hiya, Dad! See that?" he greeted him. "I was hoping you might forget to come and pick me up. We were just starting to get good at this."

Chapter Three

The next soccer practice at school was also devoted to shooting skills.

They used skittles and cones
as targets, besides trying to beat
Hannah in goal. One group
even had to try and shoot
through hoops dangling from a
crossbar.

Tom and Jonty were working together again. The captain passed the ball to his partner and Jonty steered a shot carefully through the narrow gap between two cones.

"Goal!" he whooped as the ball was collected on the other side of the cones by Imran and Michael for their turn.

"Looks like you've been putting in some more practice against the garage wall," Tom smirked.

Jonty didn't deny it. "Think I'll ask Becky if she wants to come and shoot at the boxes."

"Bet she'd jump at the chance if your dad was there too. The Red Fox is her hero!"

Jonty suddenly had to duck to avoid the ball parting his ginger hair.

"Soz!" shouted Michael. "Hit that one a bit too high."

"It nearly knocked your head off!" laughed Imran.

Tom ran to fetch the ball. "I'll get them back for you," he promised. "I'm gonna really whack this."

He lashed the ball at the goal with his right foot, but it whistled wide of the cones like a stray bullet. Michael had to set off on the chase.

"Fantastic!" cried Jonty. "What a strike!"

"Yeah, but look where it went. Power's no good without accuracy."

Michael dribbled the ball back towards them. "That bloke over there says he wants a word with you, Jonty," he said, pointing towards the fence.

Jonty peered at the man in a long dark coat. "Don't know why. I've never seen him before."

"I have," said Tom. "I've noticed him hanging about during our last couple of games. I'd watch it, if I were you."

Jonty heeded his friend's warning and stayed with the group. When he glanced over at the fence a minute later, the man was striding off along the footpath and passed out of sight behind the hedge.

"Wonder what that was all about?" he murmured to himself, puzzled, just as Sergeant Curtis arrived on the scene.

"Your dad's here, Tom," Imran called out. "Perhaps he's come to arrest Mrs Roberts!"

Tom shook his head. "Nah, I only tell him to do that when we've got a spelling test!"

★

Sergeant Curtis was at the school again the following day — on business. As the village policeman, he often came in to talk to the children about such important subjects as road safety and stranger-danger.

"No matter what reason anyone might give to try and make you get into their car, don't believe it," he reminded them. "If you don't know them, don't go with them."

His visit was very well timed. It made Jonty more suspicious about the man by the fence.

"Funny how he disappeared when Tom's dad turned up yesterday," he said to Michael back in the classroom.

Michael gave a shrug. "Probably just a coincidence. He might only have wanted to ask you for the Red Fox's autograph."

Jonty sighed. That was the trouble. Being the son of a rich pop star could have its drawbacks. It wasn't always easy to trust people. Even his dad sometimes needed bodyguards to protect him from the crowds on tour.

Jonty decided to tell Mrs Roberts what had happened and she took it far more seriously than Michael seemed to be doing.

"Sergeant Curtis hasn't left yet," she said. "Let's go and see him."

Chapter Four

"C'mon, you Greats! C'mon, you Greats!"

The chanting on the touchline grew louder and louder after Jonty put the Greats 3–0 ahead in their next game. Rebecca had already netted twice. Three shots – three goals. And it wasn't even half-time yet.

"Proves that practice makes perfect," she laughed in amazement. "We can't miss today."

"I reckon mine was a box 5 goal," Jonty joked. "Slid it into the bottom left-hand corner."

"Bet you can't get one in box 4," Tom challenged him. "Top right."

Jonty spent the rest of the
match trying to win the bet,
without success — but he did
manage pretend boxes 2 and 8
instead as both he and Rebecca
notched up hat-tricks!

Even Hannah scored in the
second half. She swapped places
with Imran and showed that she
was just as good at putting the
ball into the net as keeping it
out. Her goal was a beauty – a
left-foot volley that clipped the
post on its way in.

The Greats were now winning 7–1, but their captain still hadn't been able to get his own name on the scoresheet.

"Not fair," Tom muttered under his breath in frustration. "The only shots the goalie saves are mine."

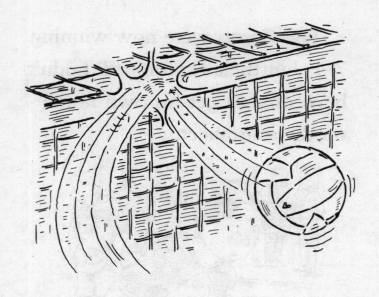

He had done everything but score. Any effort that did escape the goalie's clutches had hit the woodwork. So when the Greats were awarded a last-minute penalty, Tom quickly seized the ball.

"Captain's job," he insisted.

He blasted the penalty as hard as he could. The goalie dived out of the way to avoid being hurt, but he didn't really need to move. The ball almost went up into orbit.

It was the last kick of the
match. Tom buried his face in his
hands as Mrs Roberts blew the
final whistle. He felt so
embarrassed, he couldn't bear to
look at his teammates – and he
certainly didn't dare catch the
eye of his dad in the crowd, who
was watching out for any sign of
the stranger.

Rebecca did another of the captain's jobs for him, leading the team's "Three Cheers!" to spare Tom's blushes.

"What a game!" cried Imran. "We were brilliant."

"Apart from your goalkeeping," Michael teased him. "That was a dead soft goal you let in."

Tom was too busy sulking to join in the fun. All he wanted to do was go home. He ran off into school to grab his bag and came out of the building as Jonty reached the playground ahead of the others.

"Doesn't matter who scores the goals," Jonty told him. "The team won and that's the main thing. Your luck will change soon, you'll see."

Just at that moment, a car screeched to a halt by the school gate.

"Quick, Jonty, dive in," cried the driver, throwing open the passenger door. "The Red Fox has been in a crash. You must get to the hospital fast."

Jonty hesitated, confused, as the driver jumped out. "C'mon, there's no time to waste. Your dad's calling out for you."

Jonty began to panic, not knowing what to do, but Tom suddenly realized who the man was — the one who'd been lurking by the fence.

"No, Jonty, don't go," he shrieked. "It's a trick."

Before Jonty could react, the man lunged at him. "Got you!" he hissed, dragging him towards the car. "Your dad's gonna have to pay a lot of money if he ever wants to see you again!"

Other people saw what was
happening and broke into a run,
but Tom was the only one near
enough to do anything about it.
He used the first weapon that
came to hand – or at least to
feet – a football.

A ball sat on the playground in front of him as if perched on the penalty spot. Tom didn't have time to think. He just gave the ball a fierce thump and it sped towards its target like a guided missile.

"Box 3!" he yelled. "Bang in the middle."

The kidnapper never even saw it coming. He was trying to cram the struggling Jonty into the car when the ball struck him powerfully on the head. The force of the impact jerked him forward and his face crunched against the car roof, teeth first.

Jonty wriggled free but there was no escape for the dazed kidnapper. Sergeant Curtis pounced on him to make the arrest before the man could recover.

"Well done, son, I'm proud of you," he said, slapping Tom on the back. "I didn't think this guy was going to show up today."

"Th . . . thanks, Tom," said
Jonty shakily. "Great shot!"

"Yeah, better late than never,
I guess," Tom grinned. "Looks
like I found my shooting boots
just in time."

THE END

GREAT HIT!

Chapter One

"Brill!" cried Tom, the team captain. "Best goal of the match."

Tom wrapped his arm round the scorer's slim shoulders. "Don't know how you put so much bend on the ball," he grinned.

"Nor do I," Rebecca admitted.
"I just hit it."

The beaten goalkeeper booted
the ball away in disgust. He

thought he'd had the shot well
covered until the ball swerved
out of his reach.

"No idea what the score is
now," he muttered. "I've lost
count."

The score was even worse
than his maths. Rebecca's second
goal had put Great Catesby 9–2
ahead. The Greats were living
up to the name on the back of
their red shirts.

"We want ten!" chanted the
home fans. "We want ten!"

"C'mon, men," shouted Tom, ignoring the fact that there were two girls in the team of six. "There's still enough time to make it double figures."

The first of the Greats to touch the ball again, however, was goalkeeper Hannah – and that was only to pick it out of the tangled netting. The long-range shot had taken her by surprise and the ball skidded underneath her diving body.

The captain was not best pleased. "That was sloppy, men!" Tom moaned. "C'mon, concentrate! The game's not over till the final whistle."

A minute later, it ended in the same way as it had begun – with another goal by top-scorer Jonty.

The keeper dived to his right to make a good save, but he couldn't hold on to the ball. Jonty pounced on the rebound, stretching out a leg to poke the ball into the net.

"Goal!" he cried. "That's my fourth!"

"And it's also number thirteen in the match," said Tom, ruffling Jonty's ginger hair in delight. "Unlucky for some."

"Huh!" grunted the keeper. "More unlucky for me than you, I'd say."

*

"Ten-three!" exclaimed Michael
in the boys' cloakroom afterwards. "That's got to be some
kind of record."

"I'm more interested in the record we're making tomorrow," said Imran, Michael's partner in defence. "Hey, Jonty-boy! What time's your dad wanting us in the morning?"

Jonty reddened. He didn't like anybody but his dad calling him by that name.

"About ten o'clock," he replied. "You know that."

"Yeah, I was just wondering whether he'll be up by then," Imran laughed. "I didn't think pop stars got out of bed till the afternoon!"

Jonty's dad was better known as the Red Fox. The famous singer had recently moved into Great Catesby and he was going to record a special song with the children. Everyone hoped it would raise enough money to help save the little village school from being closed.

Tom started to chant the song's chorus and the others quickly joined in, their voices bouncing off the walls.

"C'mon, you Greats! C'mon you Greats!
Come and watch us win our games,
Come and shout out all our names.
C'mon, you Greats! C'mon you Greats!"

"Cor! It doesn't half echo around in here!" laughed Michael.

"It'll sound much better
tomorrow," said Jonty.

"Bound to, y'know, in a
proper recording studio like your
dad's had built at the Manor,"
Tom pointed out.

"I didn't mean that," Jonty grinned. "I meant the girls will be with us then – and they can sing much better than you noisy lot!"

Chapter Two

The next morning, Mrs Roberts
led the footballers and members
of the school choir through the
village towards the Manor.

"Keep up at the back there,"
the teacher called out towards
Imran's group of stragglers. "We
don't want to be late."

"Won't matter," he said. "Bet the Red Fox won't even be up yet."

Michael chuckled. "Perhaps the studio's in his bedroom!"

The jokers were in for a
surprise. The Red Fox himself
greeted the party at the iron
gates of the old Manor – fully
dressed – before showing them
towards a low, modern building
in the grounds.

"Magic!" breathed Rebecca, a big fan of the Red Fox, as she stepped inside and gazed around the studio in wonder. "This is like a dream come true. It's just too incredible for words."

"I hope not," hissed Tom. "Cos we've now got to start singing them!"

They listened first to the music that had already been recorded by the Red Fox's own band, the Earthlings.

"So what do you reckon?" he asked.

"Brill!"

"Magic!"

"Great!"

"It's perfect!" smiled Mrs Roberts. "Thanks so much."

"No trouble, lovely lady,"
replied the Red Fox, making
everyone laugh at the way he
spoke to their teacher. "Let's just
hope it does the trick."

"Course it will," said Jonty
confidently. "So now let's get the
words on that tape as well, Dad,
OK?"

"OK, you're the boss!" grinned the Red Fox, breaking into song.

"It's great, boy, it's great,
Feeling part of a team."

The pop star and his son then formed a duet to sing the rest of the first verse.

"Playing towards the
same goal,
Working together —
sharing a dream."

As arranged, the Red Fox
sang the second verse with
Rebecca as his partner. She was
feeling so nervous, her voice
sounded a little squeaky, but it
didn't matter. This was only a
practice.

> *"It's great, girl, it's great,*
> *Being on the same side.*
> *Whether we win, lose or draw,*
> *Whatever the score — knowing we*
> *tried."*

Everyone joined in the chorus and then the pattern was repeated with the next two verses. This time, though, the Red Fox sang along with all the boys, followed by all the girls.

It took the rest of the day to rehearse and get everything right, stopping only for a short picnic lunch outside in the autumn sunshine.

"Phew!" breathed Imran, chewing on a sandwich. "Didn't know making a record could be such hard work."

"Practice makes perfect," said Tom. "Just like with soccer. You have to try and make all that work in training pay off in a real match."

Chapter Three

The Greats' next practice turned
out to be rather different than
normal. They were performing
their soccer skills in front of lots
of cameras to gain extra publicity
for their fund-raising.

The Fox Cubs, as the record company called them, were not only going to appear on the CD case, but also have their pictures in the newspapers and on local television!

The Red Fox joined in the practice, too, but he was clearly a much better singer than a footballer. He kept tripping up over the ball and his snazzy tracksuit was soon covered in mud.

"Hope they don't put that one
of me in the papers," he laughed
as the photographers snapped
him missing an open goal.

"Never mind, Dad, you can't be a star at everything," grinned Jonty.

"You will be, Jonty-boy — that's for sure," said the Red Fox, slapping his son on the back. "On and off the pitch."

All the fuss that the Greats
were receiving did not go down
too well with some people. Tom's
cousin Jack, who lived in the
nearby town of Kilthorpe, was
green with envy when he saw
the Greats playing football on
television.

"You lot looked rubbish!" Jack scoffed when the Curtis family had a weekend get-together soon afterwards. "And you can't even sing."

Tom laughed it off. "You're just jealous!"

"Rubbish!" snorted Jack, using his favourite word again. "The Red Fox should've come to our school if he wanted to film some decent footballers. We could thrash you lot any day."

"No chance!"
"Oh, yeah?"
"Yeah!"
"Right," Jack decided. "Guess we'll just have to prove it, then . . ."

First thing on Monday morning, the cousins both asked their teachers if a challenge match could be arranged between the two schools. Only neither of them put it quite like that. Tom called it a 'friendly'.

"An excellent idea!" beamed
Mrs Roberts. "If the worst comes
to the worst and our school does
have to close, at least you will
have had the chance to meet
some of your future classmates."

Mr Savage, the Kilthorpe Primary sports teacher, thought it was a good idea too, but he insisted on playing eleven-a-side.

This caused Mrs Roberts a couple of problems. Firstly, she wasn't sure if there were as many as eleven children in her small class who were really up to standard. And secondly, they didn't have that many shirts.

A fortnight later, after several extra practice sessions, the Greats did manage to raise a full team – just – but only by including the Berry twins, Stephen and Rachel (or Strawberry and Raspberry, as they were better known). What the twins lacked in footballing ability, they made up for in stamina. They could both keep running all day.

172

Mr Savage solved the other
snag by digging out some tatty,
reddish tops from his own
school's P.E. store for the five
extra players to wear.

Sadly, the game did not start well for the Greats. Not used to playing on such a big pitch, their defence had almost as many holes in it as Strawberry's shirt.

Hannah came to her team's rescue in the very first minute, making a fine save right on the goal-line.

But the keeper had no chance
with the next shot. The ball
struck Michael's shoulder and
looped up into the top corner of
the net well out of her reach.

"Wish I'd known how good
Jack's lot were," Tom muttered as
another shot clunked against
Hannah's post. "This could get
very embarrassing."

Chapter Four

The Greats had Hannah to
thank for only being 3–0 down
at half-time. It was a good job
their overworked goalkeeper was
on top form or the score would
have been much worse.

Tom glared at Strawberry. "Might help if some of us didn't keep giving the ball away to the other team," he moaned during the break.

"Not my fault," Strawberry said hotly. "It's this stupid shirt they gave me. Seems to think it's still on their side."

"Best excuse
I've ever heard,"
giggled Imran.
"A haunted
shirt!"

He didn't find it
so funny when Strawberry went
and scored at the start of the
second half – in his own goal.

Taking a huge swing
at the ball,
Strawberry some-
how sliced it over
his head to send
it spinning into
the net.

Jack mocked his cousin. "You lot are rubbish!" he taunted. "Our goalie hasn't even got his knees dirty yet."

"Plenty of time left yet to make him need a bath," Tom retorted.

"Good joke, Tom," Jack sniggered, trotting away.

"C'mon, men!"
Tom cried, shaking
his fists at his
teammates.
"Let's show
'em how we
can really play."

It was almost as if Tom had
waved a magic wand instead.

The Greats went straight up
the other end and hit back with
a surprise goal.

Raspberry and Rebecca
linked up well along the wing
and created a shooting chance
for Jonty. He fired the ball low
and hard towards the target and it
slithered wide of the goalkeeper's
dive into the corner of the net.

The Greats were too busy celebrating to notice how muddy the goalie's knees were now when he stood up.

Unfortunately, Jonty's effort was not to spark off any fairy-tale revival. That tends to happen only in storybooks.

The two cousins soon knew
that they weren't imagining
things when they jumped for the
ball together and clashed heads
in mid-air. The pain was too
real for it to be make-believe.

"You've got a hard nut," Tom
said, gently touching the lump
on his forehead. "Felt like I'd
been hit by a cannonball!"

Dazed, Tom and Jack were led off the pitch to recover on the touchline. The Greats didn't have the luxury of a substitute so they were now 4–1 behind and also a player short.

To their credit, the Greats did score a second goal when Rebecca netted from close range, but they couldn't prevent Kilthorpe increasing their total. The Killers, as they were nicknamed, shot a fifth past Hannah and then added another in injury time to make it six.

"Easy! Easy!" Jack taunted his cousin after the final whistle. "The Killers murdered you!"

"We'll play you again next term when we've had a bit more practice at this eleven-a-side lark," said Tom. "Then we'll see who comes out on top."

"Huh!" Jack snorted. "You've got as much chance of doing that as your rubbish song has of being top of the pops!"

As the players trudged off the pitch, a phone was heard ringing and Jonty scurried over to pick up his coat from near the touch-line. To everyone's amazement, he pulled out a mobile phone and put it to his ear.

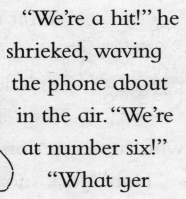

"We're a hit!" he shrieked, waving the phone about in the air. "We're at number six!"

"What yer talking about?" Michael muttered. "More like we've just been hit for six."

"Dad's just told me we're in the charts," Jonty cried. "*C'mon, you Greats!* has gone straight in at number six!"

His teammates could hardly believe such amazing news at first, but then burst into the song's chorus.

C'mon, you Greats! C'mon, you Greats!
Come and watch us win our games."

The Killers began to jeer and the singing came to a halt.

"Never mind them," said Mrs Roberts. "Just remember how the second verse goes."

The two goalscorers, Jonty and Rebecca, picked up the teacher's cue and began a little duet.

"Whether we win, lose or draw, Whatever the score, knowing we tried."

Jack smirked at his cousin. "Seems like you'll have to try a

bit harder in future. The score was
six–two, remember."

Tom pretended to look puzzled.
"Sorry, don't remember that.
Must be that bang on the bonce I
had," he grinned.

"Well you still lost!" Jack insisted.

"So what?" said Tom with a shrug. "It'll just make us even more determined to beat you next time. We aim to be the best – the number one!"

THE END

GREAT
GOAL!

Chapter One

"You can't miss!"

Strawberry proved the
captain wrong. No sooner had
Tom's cry left his lips than the
striker lofted the ball over the
crossbar.

"Oh, brilliant!" Tom sneered. "First chance we get to score and you go and blast the ball into orbit."

"Not my fault," mumbled Strawberry, blushing as red as the fruit that gave Stephen Berry his nick-name. "It must have hit a bump or something."

The village recreation ground
may not have boasted the
flattest surface in the world, but
it was the only open space in
Great Catesby big enough for
an eleven-a-side game. Their
own school playing field was far
too small.

The captain was in no mood for excuses. "I notice the bumps haven't stopped them scoring four goals," he muttered.

Things might well have been a lot worse if Hannah had not been on top form in goal, and she was soon in the thick of the action again. The keeper dived

bravely among the flying boots
in a goalmouth scramble to
wrap her body around the ball.

Imran tapped her gently on
the shoulder. "OK, it's safe to get
up now," the defender said.
"They've all gone . . ."

Hannah uncurled herself like
a cat waking up from a nap in
front of the fire.

"... But they'll soon be
back," Imran added with a grin.

"Well, what do you expect?" she said, giving a shrug. "I mean, it's not that they're so much better than us. They're just bigger – and older."

"Well saved, Hannah," called out their teacher, Mrs Roberts, who was in charge of the practice match between the school's two junior classes. "Now let's see how far you can kick it."

Hannah booted the ball away
as hard as she could. It still fell
well short of the halfway line,
but at least found a teammate
on the left wing.

Rebecca hadn't touched the ball for ages and she wasn't going to waste this chance to play with it. The winger beat the first defender for sheer pace and then used her dribbling skills to outwit the second.

"Yes, Becky – to me!" cried
Tom, running up in support.

Rebecca ignored him. She
tried to dribble her way past
another player instead, but the
tackle was too strong and the
ball was lost.

"That was greedy!" Tom complained. "You should have passed."

Rebecca made no reply. She knew the captain was right.

All was forgotten and forgiven, however, a few minutes later, when Tom's team put together the best move of the match — with Rebecca supplying the final pass to their leading scorer, Jonty Fox.

Jonty flicked the ball up into the air and then volleyed it goalwards as it dropped. The keeper barely even saw the guided missile zoom past him.

It was their one moment of glory in the game. By the time Mrs Roberts called a halt, the score was 7–1 to the Top Juniors.

Tom slumped down wearily in the centre-circle. "Oh, well," he sighed. "Guess things can only get better . . ."

Chapter Two

Two days later, the headteacher had some wonderful news for the young children of Great Catesby.

"We've won!" Miss Jackson announced in assembly. "Thanks to all your marvellous efforts, our lovely little school is now saved!"

The children clapped and
cheered. The village school had
been in danger of closure until
the success of their recent
money-raising activities. The last
thing they'd wanted was to be
bussed into the nearby town of
Kilthorpe to attend the big
school there.

"Let's sing our special song to celebrate," said Miss Jackson.

This was the song that the pupils had recorded with a famous pop star, the Red Fox – otherwise known to them as Jonty's dad.

They didn't even wait for the headteacher to reach the piano before bursting into the chorus.

> "*C'mon, you Greats! C'mon, you Greats!*
> *Come and watch us win our games.*
> *Come and shout out all our names.*
> *C'mon, you Greats! C'mon, you Greats!*"

"I'm glad to hear you're in such fine voice," Miss Jackson laughed, settling herself at the piano. "Because I've had a most amazing telephone call this morning. The TV people want us to appear on *Chart Chasers*!"

The children were too stunned to react at first. *Chart Chasers* was their favourite programme on pop music.

Then the old school building was almost in need of some emergency repair work. The huge explosion of cheers nearly blew the hall roof off!

The coach from Great Catesby
was delayed in the heavy
London traffic and the children
were late arriving at the
television studio.

The Red Fox was already there. "Hi, gang!" he greeted them. "Glad you made it at last. Beginning to think you might have chickened out!"

"No chance of that, Dad," Jonty laughed. "Not the Greats."

Many of his teammates,
however, and also their friends
in the school choir *were* feeling a
bit nervous. Some had even been
sick on the journey, but tried to
blame it on the swaying of the
coach.

"This is so *incredible!*" breathed Hannah, her voice almost a whisper. "I can hardly believe we're really inside the *Chart Chasers* studio."

"Magic!" exclaimed Rebecca, wide-eyed with wonder. "Have you still got butterflies in your tummy?"

The goalkeeper shook her head. "Not any more. They've all flown away now we're here, just like they do when a match kicks off."

The children had the most fantastic time over the next few hours. During breaks in rehearsals with the Red Fox's band, the Earthlings, they went round collecting the autographs of as many stars as they dared to ask.

Rebecca's book was soon full, but she couldn't get over the shock of being asked for her own autograph by the drummer of a big American band.

"Like yer single, little lady," he drawled, holding out a torn piece of paper. "D'yer play as well as yer sing?"

"You mean the drums?" said Rebecca, not sure if the man was making fun of her.

"No, I mean soccer," he replied seriously. "I'd sooner play soccer than the drums any day!"

Miss Jackson and Mrs Roberts watched from behind a screen as their pupils performed on stage in the show itself in front of the cameras.

"They sound super!" cried
Mrs Roberts. "I'm so proud of
them."

The headteacher beamed.
"Best I've ever heard them sing.
They've risen to the occasion –
as always. I knew they would."

The young audience loved the song, too, dancing and swaying to the music under the studio's multi-coloured, flashing lights.

Backed by the choir, the Red
Fox sang along first with
Jonty . . .

"It's great, boy, it's great,
Feeling part of a team.
Playing towards the same goal,
Working together – sharing a
    dream."

... and then with Rebecca ...

"It's great, girl, it's great,
Being on the same side.
Whether we win, lose or draw,
Whatever the score — knowing we
    tried."

The fans whooped and clapped loudly when the final chorus of the song ended and the children felt almost in a daze backstage afterwards.

"You were all GREAT!" cried the Red Fox in delight. "With a bit of luck, kids, I reckon we might even be the new Christmas number one!"

Chapter Three

The Red Fox was proved right.
C'mon, you Greats was indeed top
of the charts on Christmas Day.

Tom celebrated their hit
record in the best way that he
knew how – by playing football.

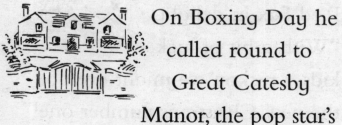

On Boxing Day he
called round to
Great Catesby
Manor, the pop star's

country home, to have some extra shooting practice with Jonty.

"Made cousin Jack watch a tape of the TV show yesterday after Christmas dinner," Tom chuckled as he set himself up for yet another shot. "He went all green."

"Perhaps he'd eaten too much turkey!" Jonty grinned.

"Jealousy, more like," Tom smirked. "Bet Jack can't wait till we play his Killers again next term so he can try and get his own back."

"It's *us* who are out for revenge," Jonty reminded him. "The Killers won the first game."

The captain pulled a face. He preferred to forget that Kilthorpe Primary School had beaten the Greats in a challenge match before Christmas.

Tom belted the ball at the goal they'd drawn on a garage wall. The target was divided up into eight numbered squares, but he missed the lot.

Jonty laughed and scampered after the rebound to have his next turn. He pretended that he was taking a penalty and struck the ball firmly into the bottom right-hand corner of the goal.

"Box eight –
the winner!" he
cried.

"Huh! Lucky."

"Which one were you on?"
Jonty asked cheekily.

"Four," he grunted. "As if you
didn't know."

"Shame!" Jonty giggled. "All
this fame must be going to your
head."

"Watch it or I'll see this ball
goes straight to yours,"
Tom warned him. "I sure
won't miss something
the size of that."

"Oh, yeah?" Jonty taunted. "You couldn't even hit a barn door."

Tom pounced on the ball and Jonty realized that the captain meant business. He ran off towards the main building, with Tom dribbling the ball after him in hot pursuit.

When Jonty slipped on a wet patch of grass on the front lawn, Tom seized his chance and let fly. He struck the ball powerfully in his stride, but Jonty saw it coming just in time and ducked out of the way.

The window wasn't so lucky.

CRASH!!

The boys stared at the broken pane of glass in horror.

"Quick, let's leg it," gasped Tom.

They weren't fast enough. The Red Fox's housekeeper came scuttling out of the front door and grabbed Jonty by the arm.

"You and your football!" she cried. "I'll see the cost of this window comes out of your pocket money, young man."

Tom resisted the natural urge to run away. "Um, actually it was my fault," he admitted. "I kicked the ball."

The woman glared at him. "Well, you can sweep up all the glass, then," she said. "Go and fetch him a brush and dustpan, Jonty."

Tom was set to work under close supervision. The house-keeper made sure every tiny piece of glass was picked up, inside and out.

Jonty couldn't resist a joke at his pal's expense. "Looks like you'd make a good sweeper!" he giggled.

Tom's face suddenly lit up. "Hey! Thanks, Jonty," he grinned. "You've just gone and given me a wicked idea for how we might beat the Killers!"

Tom explained his new tactics to Mrs Roberts on the very first day back at school in the New Year. "You want us to change to a sweeper system?" said the teacher, looking puzzled.

"I doubt whether many of the team would know how it works. I'm not even sure that I do."

"It's worth a try, Mrs Roberts," he pleaded. "We can hardly do any worse than last time."

"Well, that's true," she agreed, nodding. "OK, then, captain, we'll give it a go – as long as you play the role of sweeper."

Tom grinned. "Great!" he exclaimed. "I've already been getting in some practice during the holidays!"

Chapter Four

"Right, men," said Tom, addressing his mixed team of eight boys and three girls before the match. "Now we're top of the charts, let's go and show them Killers who's best at football too."

The Greats even had a full set of kit to wear at last. The Red Fox had given the school a Christmas present of six more red and white soccer strips.

The pop star was standing on the touchline as the players ran onto the Kilthorpe pitch to warm up.

"C'mon, you Greats!" he sang to greet them.

Five minutes after the kick-off, the Red Fox was jumping about even more than he did on stage.

Jonty had just put the Greats 1–0 ahead.

It was a brilliant goal. Raspberry, Strawberry's twin sister, slipped Jonty the ball just outside the Killers' penalty area and he drove it high into the roof of the net.

The Greats did well to hold their slim lead for most of the first half. The Killers were a very good team, but it took them a long time to break down the Greats' sweeper system.

Tom had been outstanding in his new position, dealing with any passes that beat the other defenders. His favourite moment came when he swept the ball away off Jack's toes just as his cousin looked certain to score.

But even Tom could not prevent the Killers from equalizing with a header and then going 2–1 up just before half-time.

A cross from the left wing evaded Hannah's grasp and Jack had a simple tap-in goal at the far post.

"It was only a matter of time," Jack whooped. "We'll walk it now, easy!"

"No way!" Tom retorted. "The Greats never give up."

Tom was right about that, but they still had Hannah to thank for not falling further behind straight after the break. She deflected a long-range effort against a post and then scrambled to her feet in time to smother the rebound. It was a superb double save.

As the minutes ticked by, Tom decided to push forward into midfield to try and keep the ball more in the Killers' half of the pitch. He crunched into a tackle to win the ball and curled a pass out to Rebecca.

 The winger linked
up well with Jonty, but
Strawberry failed to
control her cross and the home
side were able to clear the danger.

The Greats now began to
dominate the match. They
missed two more good chances
to score, but when the equalizer
finally came, it was well worth
waiting for.

The Berry twins
exchanged passes
neatly with each
other before Strawberry
slid the ball forward to Rebecca.

She didn't need any more help. Glancing up, she saw the goalkeeper had advanced off his line to narrow the shooting angle. So Rebecca chipped the ball over his head instead.

Everyone watched the flight of the ball. It looked to be floating over the bar at first, but then it dipped and dropped into the top corner of the net.

"C'mon, men!" yelled Tom. "We can win this now." They did exactly that, but even Tom had to admit that he left it late. The captain was having the game of his young life, charging up and down the pitch to support both defence and attack.

And he was in the right place at the right time – the very last minute of the game – to hit the winning goal.

Rebecca's pass found him unmarked on the edge of the Killers' penalty area and Tom smacked the ball goalwards as hard as he could.

The keeper flung out an arm to try and block the shot, but it seemed almost as if he was waving the ball goodbye. It flashed into the net to make the final score 3–2 to the Greats.

The cousins shook hands after the final whistle.

"No hard feelings?" said Tom.

"No hard feelings," replied Jack, forcing a smile. "And no excuses either. You beat us fair and square today."

"Well played, everybody," said
Mrs Roberts as the Greats
gathered around their teacher.
"I'm really proud of you."

The Red Fox joined the
group too. "Great stuff, kids!" he
grinned. "Happy New Year!"

They could all look forward
to a Happy New Year now and
to playing many more games of
football together as well. The
school was saved and the future
looked as bright as the Red
Fox's long red hair.

"*C'mon, you Greats!*" they sang
loudly. "*C'mon, you Greats!*"

THE END

STRIKE!

Rob Childs

In the net!

Missed! Whether it's football or fishing,
Jake seems to be out of luck. He can't get a
ball *or* a fish into the net! Adam and Owen are
very keen to help Jake score – but will their deal
mean Jake has to keep his 'fishy' promise?

Corgi Pups are perfect for new readers
just starting out on real books.

ISBN 0 552 55031 0

Rob Childs

What a wicked day!

Join in all the fun and games of Sports Day.
Bradley and his mates are out to make it a very
special day. But why can't Jagdish take part?
What's happened to the Cup? And why does the
school's grumpy old caretaker think it's a dog's life?

On your marks – Get set – Go!

A SPORTS SPECIAL STORY

Corgi Pups are perfect for new readers
just starting out on real books.

ISBN 0 552 54791 3

WicKEd Catch!

Rob Childs

Catches win Matches!

Come and enjoy all the fun and drama of
a special challenge game of rounders. It's class
against class, brother versus brother, and everybody
sees red! What goes up must come down – but
who wants to be underneath a high dropping ball
to make a vital catch? Well, Bradley's dog,
Dylan, does for a start... Woof!

Rounder! Rounder! Rounder!

A SPORTS SPECIAL STORY

Corgi Pups are perfect for new readers
just starting out on real books.

ISBN 0552 547921